THOMAS' Railway Word Book

Illustrated by Paul Nichols

bird — dome — whistle — tender — wheel arch

Random House 🏠 New York

A Random House PICTUREBACK® Book

Thomas the Tank Engine & Friends

A BRITT ALLCROFT COMPANY PRODUCTION

Based on The Railway Series by the Rev W Awdry. Copyright © Gullane (Thomas) LLC 2000. All rights reserved under International and Pan-American Copyright Conventions. Published in the United States by Random House, Inc., New York, and simultaneously in Canada by Random House of Canada Limited, Toronto.
www.randomhouse.com/kids   www.thomasthetankengine.com

ISBN 0-375-80281-9

Library of Congress Catalog Card Number: 00-100733
Printed in the United States of America   November 2000   20 19 18 17 16 15 14 13 12 11

porthole

Percy pushes a **freight car** to James.
James' **coupling hook** connects to the **coupling chain**.

logs

coupling hook

buffer

5

freight car

coupling chain

James holds coal in a special bin called a **tender**.
He uses his **whistle** to talk to a **bird**.

dome

whistle

bird

The **porter** puts a **suitcase** on the train. A **passenger** walks to the **coach**.

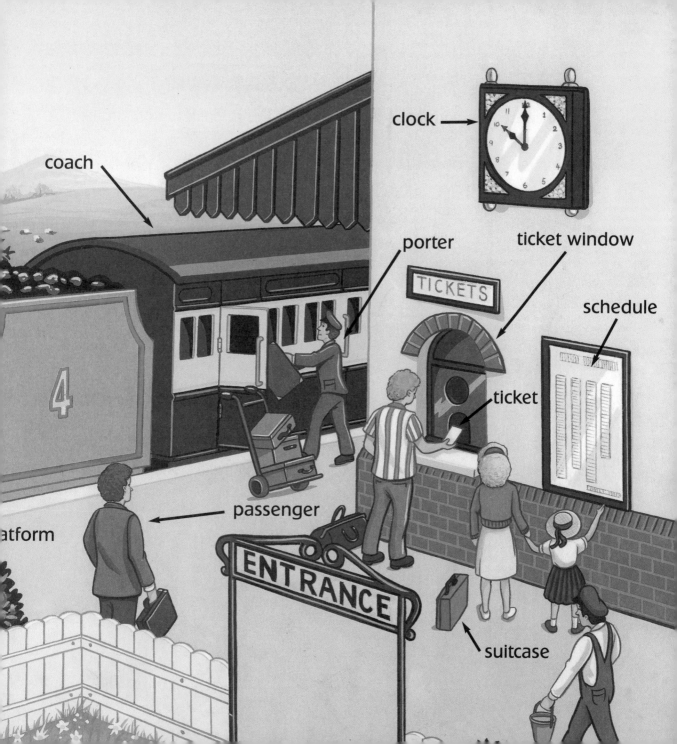

coach

clock

porter

ticket window

schedule

TICKETS

ticket

passenger

atform

ENTRANCE

suitcase

4

Henry has had an accident.
The **breakdown train** uses a **crane** to lift Henry back onto the track.

hook

sheep

hay bale

flatbed car

crane

cable

breakdown train

windmill

driver

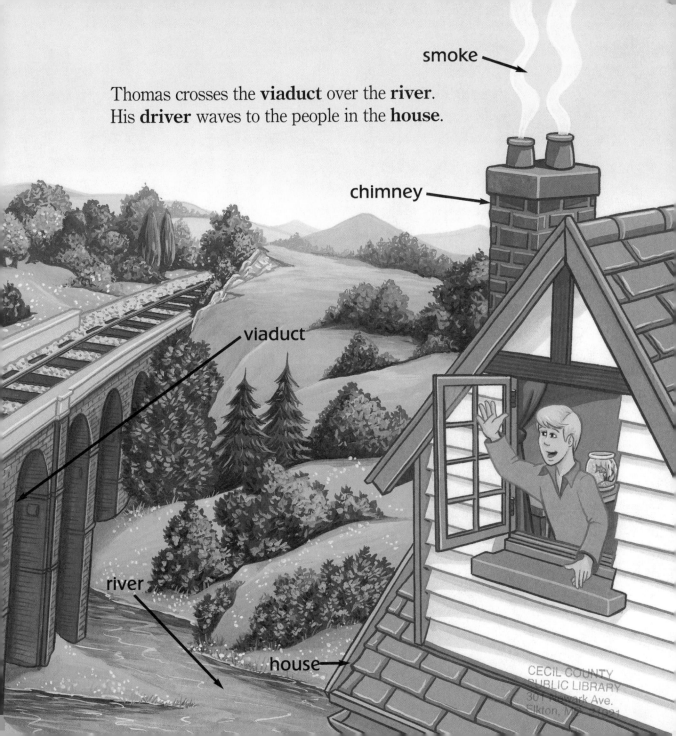

smoke

Thomas crosses the **viaduct** over the **river**.
His **driver** waves to the people in the **house**.

chimney

viaduct

river

house

bricks

tunnel

tracks

wheels

Snow makes Thomas' **wheels** slip.
He uses his **snowplow** to clear the **tracks**.

mountain

snow

snowplow

Mavis and Thomas meet at the junction.
Mavis is a **diesel engine** pulling a load of **gravel**.

flag

guard

steps

gravel

signal

diesel engine

MAVIS

THE FFARQUHAR QUARRY CO. LTD.

mast

fish

boat

dock

James picks up **fish** at the **dock**.
A **sailor** ties up his **boat** with a strong **rope**.

helicopter

ilor

rope

seagull

ladder

Thomas' tank is filled with **water** from the **water tower**.

steam

water tower

water

pipe

1

wheel arch

firebox

Heat from the **firebox** turns the water to **steam**.

fireman

coal

shovel

Toby is an old-fashioned **tram engine**.
Instead of a whistle, he has a **bell**.

cow

bus

tram engine

wooden panel

bell

7

cowcatcher

Gordon spins around on the **turntable**.

fence

funnel

handrail

turntable

The trains rest in the **shed** at night.

moon

shed

star

Thomas

James

Henry

Percy

Gordon

Thomas' **lamp** sits on his **lamp rod**. Good night, Thomas.

lamp rod

lamp

brake pipe